GLADYS THE MAGIC CHICKEN

by ADAM RUBIN

Illustrated by ADAM REX

putnam

G. P. PUTNAM'S SONS

For Gary Larson, without whom this book would probably be about a cuddly bunny.
—A. Rubin

For Maurice Noble (1911–2001). Look him up.
—A. Rex

G. P. PUTNAM'S SONS
An imprint of Penguin Random House LLC, New York

Text copyright © 2021 by Adam Rubin
Illustrations copyright © 2021 by Adam Rex
G. P. Putnam's Sons is a registered trademark of Penguin Random House LLC.

Visit us online at penguinrandomhouse.com

Library of Congress Cataloging-in-Publication Data is available.

Manufactured in China by RR Donnelley Asia Printing Solutions Ltd.
ISBN 9780593325605
10 9 8 7 6 5 4 3 2 1

Design by Marikka Tamura & Adam Rex
Text set in Triplex Sans OT
This book was drawn and painted digitally.

THIS ALL HAPPENED

a long, long, long, long, looong time ago.

Three thousand years before your grandma's

grandma's grandma was born.

We call it Ancient Times.

And in Ancient Times, they talked like this:

LO AND BEHOLD HOW THIS CHICKEN DOTH DANCE AFTER FEASTING!

See that dancing chicken, kid? That's our hero.
That there is Gladys.

EVERY DAY,

Gladys followed the sheep,
who followed the dog,
who followed the Shepherd Boy
through the mountain pass.

The Shepherd Boy worked all day and never went to school, because in Ancient Times, school had not been invented yet. (It's true—look it up.)

Well, the Shepherd Boy?
He never learned how
to look things up
or how to read or write
or know science,
so understandably,
he was not nearly as
smart as you are.

For instance, one day the Shepherd Boy found a puddle, which he thought was a hole in the ground with an upside-down boy inside.

To be fair, the Shepherd Boy had never seen his own reflection before, and after a few minutes of waving, he did eventually realize he was looking at himself. He was horrified.

MISERY AND WOE! I'M HIDEOUS!

cried
the Shepherd Boy suddenly,
which frightened Gladys,
who plooped out an egg.

PLOOP

He wept and wailed and pounded his fists
in the mud. Gladys nuzzled the boy's neck
to comfort him.

OH, GLADYS,

sighed
the Shepherd Boy,

I WISH THAT I WERE BEAUTIFUL.

YEARS PASSED and the Shepherd Boy changed. His arms became thick, and his chestnut hair fell past his shoulders. He grew strong wrestling the sheep to give them haircuts—shepherds call it "shearing," but sheep call it

‿BAAAAAAAA!

That strapping Shepherd Boy could shear a sheep in sixty-seven seconds flat. Though, it should be noted, clocks had not been invented yet in Ancient Times.

One day, a Traveling Merchant came to the mountains.
His wagon was full of treasures from faraway lands:

spices
(the Shepherd Boy
had never tasted pepper),

fabrics
(the Shepherd Boy
had never touched silk),
and, rarest of all,

a shiny,
polished
looking
glass.

Well, heck—the Shepherd Boy
hadn't seen his reflection
since all those years before
in that muddy puddle, so
at first, the handsome face
in the mirror startled him.
But this time, it only took
him one wave to figure it out.

The Shepherd Boy was overjoyed.
He scooped up Gladys and kissed her
smack on the beak. This confused
the Traveling Merchant, who had seen
many strange things in his travels but
none quite as odd as a shepherd
smooching a chicken.

"GLADYS HATH GRANTED
MY WISH TO BE BEAUTIFUL!"
declared the Shepherd Boy.
"'TIS A MAGIC CHICKEN—A MAGIC,
WISH-GRANTING CHICKEN."
This intrigued the Traveling Merchant.
He proposed a trade.

And that's how the Traveling Merchant wound up riding away with Gladys in his wagon, while the Shepherd Boy was left with a shiny new looking glass in which to admire himself.

 **GLADYS** had never been down from the mountains before.
She'd never seen the shimmering sea;
she'd never heard the wind whip through the wheat;
she'd never smelled a tired old donkey.

MAGIC CHICKEN!

GET YER MAGIC CHICKEN HERE!
EVERY WISH GRANTED!
RESPONDS TO GLADYS!
NO WISHING PRIOR TO PURCHASE!

The Traveling Merchant shouted till his throat was sore. The villagers in the market bought magic stones and magic bones, but for some reason, none of them believed a chicken could be magic.

I WISH I WAS RID OF THIS STINKIN' CHICKEN,

muttered the Traveling Merchant as he packed up his wares.

And just like that—he realized that Gladys was gone.

A Long-Bearded Bandit had stolen Gladys away and was planning to eat her for dinner.

"YE BE A 'MAGIC CHICKEN,' EH, GLADYS?" chuckled the Long-Bearded Bandit as he lit a fire under his pot. "WELL, I WISH TO VISIT THE PALACE OF THE PURPLE POOH-BAH!"

The Long-Bearded Bandit laughed and laughed,
a little too loudly, actually, because a Brave Swordsman
overheard the commotion and decided to investigate.

HARK! THIEF!
FROM WHENCE DID YE
PILFER THIS CHICKEN?

The Brave Swordsman deftly disarmed the Long-Bearded Bandit and
bound him with rope. He rescued Gladys. Then he carried the thief
to the palace of the Purple Pooh-bah
and threw him in the dungeon.

cried the Long-Bearded Bandit.

A sudden blast of trumpets startled the Brave Swordsman.
But not as much as Gladys, who plooped out
an egg that went *splat* on his shoe.

PLOOP

Flower girls threw petals, musicians played and danced, and the soldiers of the Royal Guard marched in perfect unison as they carried the Purple Pooh-bah toward the palace.

To march in the Royal Guard was the greatest wish of the Brave Swordsman. So when the Purple Pooh-bah passed by, he puffed up his chest to look as brave as possible.

PARDON ME, BRAVE SWORDSMAN, said the Purple Pooh-bah, BUT WHY DOST THOU CARRY A CHICKEN?

The Brave Swordsman blushed and bowed. "'TIS SAID TO BE A MAGIC CHICKEN, YOUR HIGHNESS."

The Purple Pooh-bah chuckled. He was always skeptical of any so-called "magic," but there was something undeniably amusing about that chicken.

He decided she would make an excellent gift for his daughter, the Learned Princess (who, by the way, had become learned thanks to private tutors—remember, there were no schools in Ancient Times).

In exchange for the chicken, the Brave Swordsman
was invited to join the Royal Guard,
just as he had wished.

THANK YOU, GLADYS,

he called as the Purple Pooh-bah carried her away.

THE PURPLE POOH-BAH had a thriving kingdom, a lovely palace, and a vault full of magnificent jewels, but all he really wanted was for his only daughter to be happy.

When the Purple Pooh-bah opened the Learned Princess's door, she hurled an urn past his head. It smashed to pieces against the wall—which is a shame, really, because nowadays an urn from Ancient Times would be worth a million dollars, at least.

"I OFFER A GIFT," protested the Purple Pooh-bah. "'TIS A MAGIC CHICKEN NAMED GLADYS!"

GET OUT OF MY ROOM!

screamed the Learned Princess.

The Purple Pooh-bah
left the chicken,
shut the door, and
dusted the bits of
urn from his robe.
"TEENAGERS . . ."
He shook his head.

And that's how Gladys went from pecking through sheep dung to living in the royal palace.

When Gladys first tried a fig, she danced a boogie so vigorous that it tickled the Learned Princess to tears.

The Purple Pooh-bah heard his daughter's laughter echoing through the halls of the palace, and he had to wonder if maybe the chicken really was magic.

The Learned Princess spent all her time reading scrolls.
(They did not have books in Ancient Times.)
She longed to explore the wide world,
which she had read so much about,
but her tutors feared for her safety,
so they kept her locked in her room.

The only one who brought her joy
was Gladys, so she wrote her a song:

GLAAAAADYS THE MAAAAAGIC CHIIIICKEN, ABRA-COCK-A-DOODLE-DEE-DOO!

The tune was a very catchy little ditty,
and soon everyone in the kingdom
was singing it.

But while Gladys gladly gobbled figs,
the Learned Princess gazed out her window
at the shimmering sea and sighed. Her
real wish was to escape from the palace.

The Learned Princess shrieked as a Fearsome Pirate swung through the window, flipped through the air, and landed on the floor with a sword clenched in her teeth. Gladys let an egg go *ploop*.

"YOU'RE COMING WITH ME," threatened the Fearsome Pirate. "I'M HERE TO KIDNAP YOU FOR RANSOM!"

"HOORAY!" squealed the Learned Princess.

HOORAY? asked the Fearsome Pirate.

The Learned Princess happily packed her bags:
mostly scrolls,
a warm cloak,
and, of course, Gladys.

PLOOP

ON THE DECK of the mighty pirate ship, the crew made merry and sang songs of the sea with the Learned Princess. They fed Gladys grapes and watched her dance.

"TO ADVENTURE!" The Fearsome Pirate raised her goblet and winked at the chicken. "MAY IT FOLLOW US WHEREVER WE GO!"

Flaming arrows rained down from the sky.
The ship was under attack! Rival pirates climbed
aboard and drew their swords. A vicious fight
broke out, claiming many lives and limbs.

The Learned Princess managed to escape
thanks to the valiant efforts of the Fearsome Pirate,
but she wept as she rowed away, for her beloved
chicken was nowhere to be found . . .

(Relax, relax. Gladys was fine.
This story has a happy ending—
calm down.)

Gladys wound up perched on
the head of a Drowning Sailor,
who splashed and gasped and
thrashed through the churning
sea. (Very few people learned
proper swimming technique
back in Ancient Times.)
Eventually, the Drowning Sailor
grabbed hold of a floating
plank of wood and prayed that
he might somehow survive
to sail another day.

When the Drowning Sailor awoke, he was surprised to discover
he had not drowned after all. Gladys hopped off his head
to hunt for clams in the sand.

PRAISE BE THE MAGIC CHICKEN THAT HATH SAVED MY LIFE!

shouted the No-Longer-Drowning Sailor.
Then he coughed up a bucket of seawater,
lay down, and took a nap.

A Lone Rider heard the shouting and approached the beach to investigate. Gladys pecked a clam from its shell, slurped it down her gullet, and did her little boogie dance.

The Lone Rider smiled, which she hadn't done in a very long time. She dismounted her horse, scooped up the chicken, and decided to take her for a ride.

PLOOP

THEY RODE AWAY

from the sea, past the town,
through the fields, and up toward
the mountain pass. The horse galloped
so hard and so fast, it jostled an egg
loose from the jiggling chicken.

As they approached the foothills,
the road was blocked by a flock of sheep
in dire need of shearing.

Their Shepherd had been distracted by his desperate search for a long-lost friend.

GLADYS!

he exclaimed as he dropped to his knees.

FORGIVE ME! I SMASHED THAT CURSED LOOKING GLASS WHAT HAD CONSUMED MY MIND. HOW I WISHED UPON WISH THAT I MIGHT FIND YOU AGAIN.

The Lone Rider spied the Shepherd's sturdy form and healthy mouth.

—AND HOW I WISHED UPON WISH THAT I MIGHT FIND A WORTHY COMPANION,

she whispered to her horse.

AND SO, the No-Longer-a-Boy Shepherd
and the No-Longer-Lone Rider and the dog
and the sheep and of course Gladys made
a very happy home in the mountains.

Maybe Gladys never granted any wishes, but her song had already been written,
and the ballad was passed down from generation to generation and translated
from one language to the next, forgotten, remembered, and eventually
printed in this book so that someday you, too,
could share the story of Gladys with someone
who wishes to see magic in the world,
even if they are only looking at a chicken.

PLOOP.